A VERY FIRST PICTURE BOOK

teddies

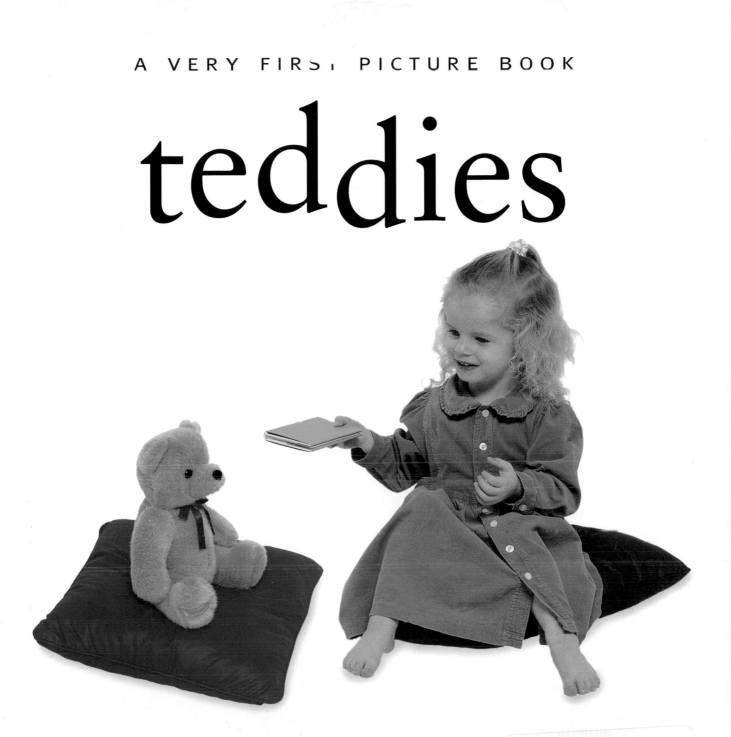

CONSULTANT: NICOLA TUXWORTH

LORENZ BOOKS

Look at all my teddy bears!

Smart bear

Grey bear

Old bear

Fluffy bear

Ginger
bear

Tartan
bear

Baby
bear

Cuddly
bear

Golden bear

One teddy
bear riding
on the
train...

... two teddy
bears riding
in the truck ...

... but how
many bears
riding in the car?

Time for
a picnic.

Look out!

Here come
the bears.

Now it's a teddy bears' picnic!

Phew! It's hot today, Teddy!

Are you
thirsty?

Time for
a snooze,
I think!

Teddies
like to
look at
books.

Shall I read
to you?

Once upon
a time ...

Listen ...

Ting
on the
triangle.

Jingle
on the
tambourine.

Peep
on the
harmonica.

Rat-a-tat-tat
on the drum.

Let's dance!

Teddy and
I are off to
the park.

Scrunch, scrunch through the autumn leaves!

Are you warm enough, Teddy?

The teddies are playing hide and seek.

Where are those bears?

Come and find me!

Peek-a-boo!

Perhaps they're over here.

We're bedtime bears!

Is there
room
for me?

Let's say
goodnight
too, Bear.

Shhh!
The bears
are asleep.

This edition published by Lorenz Books in 2002

© Anness Publishing Limited 1997, 2002

Lorenz Books is an imprint of
Anness Publishing Limited
Hermes House
88–89 Blackfriars Road
London SE1 8HA

www.lorenzbooks.com

This edition distributed in Canada by
Raincoast Books
9050 Shaughnessy Street, Vancouver
British Columbia V6P 6E5

A CIP catalogue record is available from
the British Library

Publisher: Joanna Lorenz
Senior Editor, Children's Books:
    Gilly Cameron Cooper
Special Photography: John Freeman
Design and Typesetting:
    Michael Leaman Design Partnership

The publishers would like to thank the
following children (and their parents) for
appearing in this book: Chilli Bernstein,
Mark Bloodworth, Andrew Brown, April
Cain, Freddy Cassford, Saffron George, Erin
Hoel, Philip Quach, Eloise Shepherd, Giovanni
Sipiano, Pippa Vaughan and James Xu.

10 9 8 7 6 5 4 3 2 1